Kitten Friends #1

Felix the Fluffy Kitten

by Jenny Dale
illustrated by Susan Hellard

Aladdin Paperbacks
New York   London   Toronto   Sydney   Singapore

Look for these KITTEN FRIENDS books!

#2 *Bob the Bouncy Kitten*
Coming soon

#3 *Star the Snowy Kitten*
#4 *Nell the Naughty Kitten*
#5 *Leo the Lucky Kitten*
#6 *Patch the Perfect Kitten*

Special thanks to Mary Hooper

To Maisie—a star in her own right

First Aladdin Paperbacks edition October 2000
Text copyright © 1999 by Working Partners Limited
Illustrations copyright © 1999 by Susan Hellard
First published 1999 by Macmillan Children's Books U.K.
Created by Working Partners Limited

Aladdin Paperbacks
An imprint of Simon & Schuster Children's Publishing Division
1230 Avenue of the Americas
New York, NY 10020

The text for this book was set in 16-point Palatino.
Printed and bound in the United States of America

2 4 6 8 10 9 7 5 3 1

Library of Congress Control Number: 00-107109
ISBN: 0-689-84108-6

Chapter One

Jodie Taylor woke with a start and remembered what day it was. She jumped out of bed and ran straight downstairs in her pajamas.

"Happy birthday, sleepyhead!" her mom said as Jodie bounced into the kitchen. "I was just about to come and wake you up. I can't believe you slept late today!"

"I was awake at five o'clock, wondering what presents I'd get," Jodie said, rubbing her eyes. "But then I dozed off again."

Jodie's dad came into the kitchen with his coat on. "Happy birthday, honey!" He looked at his watch. "I'll just about have time to watch you open your presents."

Jodie looked excitedly at the pile of cards and presents beside her cereal bowl. She sat down and began opening them.

There was a soft, pink sweater from her nana, a computer game from Uncle Jack, and a knapsack in the shape of a lamb from Aunt Joyce. But nothing from her mom and dad.

Jodie looked at them, surprised. Then her dad winked at her mom. What was going on?

"Now open the cards!" he said.

Jodie tore open her cards. There were eight of them—the same number as her new age.

At the bottom of the pile was an ordinary-looking brown envelope with Jodie's name on it. "This doesn't look like a card," she said.

Mr. Taylor peered at it. "It doesn't look like anything much."

"Looks like a bill," said Mrs. Taylor, trying not to smile.

Jodie opened the envelope and pulled out a small white square of paper.

On it was written:

IOU one kitten.

Jodie looked at her parents in aston-
ishment. "What does this mean?"

"It means," said Mrs. Taylor, smiling,
"that your dad and I owe you one birthday kitten—and we're going to pick it
up later."

Jodie gave a squeal of delight.

"Really?" This was what she'd dreamed of for ages. But her mom and dad had always said no. Until now!

Mr. Taylor buttoned his coat.

"Mom's taking you to see a lady named Mrs. Dent after school," he said. "She has a litter of kittens ready to go to new homes." He dropped a kiss on Jodie's head. "Got to rush. have a great day!" And he left for work.

"A kitten," Jodie breathed. "A real live kitten." She gave her mom a hug.

Mrs. Taylor smiled. She said, "Dad and I think you're old enough now to take care of a pet of your own, Jodie."

"Oh, I am, I am!" Jodie said.

"So it's up to you to look after the kitten," Mrs. Taylor went on. "You know how busy Dad and I are at the moment. We don't have time to feed and groom a pet or . . . " she made a face " . . . clean up any messes."

"Oh, there won't be any messes," Jodie said. She knew a lot about pets and loved reading stories about cats. "Kittens are really clean. They're house-trained by their mothers from the moment they're born."

"I'm glad to hear it," said Mrs. Taylor as she wiped around the sink and gave it a little extra polish. "Because you know I can't stand a mess."

Jodie was used to her mom's neat and

tidy ways and hardly heard her. She was getting a kitten! She was getting a kitten of her very own. She could hardly wait!

Chapter Two

"Oh, they're all adorable!" Jodie said as five tiny kittens played around her feet. There were three fluffy gray kittens, like their mother, and two sweet black-and-white ones with pink noses.

Jodie sighed deeply. "I'm never going to be able to choose!" She got down on the floor and picked up one kitten at a time. "Oh, I don't know!" she wailed.

Jodie's mom smiled. "Can you help, Mrs. Dent?"

"They're all good, clean little kittens," Mrs. Dent said. "But the short-haired black-and-whites would be easier to care for. The gray kittens, being long-haired, will need lots more grooming."

"Oh, I won't mind doing that," Jodie said. "I will love combing my kitten." She held up one of the gray fluffies. "This one has the bluest eyes. And he's really fluffy!"

The kitten looked at Jodie and meowed. "Choose me!"

Jodie laughed and put him down so she could look at the other kittens again. But she kept coming back to the fluffiest one.

The kitten went up to Jodie and
rubbed his face against her ankle. "You
look nice," he purred. "I'll miss my
mother and my brothers and sisters—
but I won't mind coming home with
you."

"I really think you'll have to make up

your mind, honey," Jodie's mom said. "I'm sure Mrs. Dent has other things to do."

Jodie watched as the kittens tumbled around, each trying to look the sweetest.

"Come on, Jodie," said Mrs. Taylor.

The fluffiest kitten climbed onto Jodie's sneaker, mewing up at her. And . . . well, if a kitten could smile, he was doing it.

Jodie's heart melted. "Okay, I want . . ." She took a deep breath then scooped up the fluffiest kitten. "This one! I love him already."

Delighted, the kitten pushed his head into Jodie's neck. "Good choice," he purred.

"At last!" said Mrs. Taylor.

"What are you going to call him, dear?" Mrs. Dent asked, smiling.

Jodie thought hard. "I'm going to call him Felix," she said. She cuddled Felix. "You're my fluffy Felix."

Tired from all his kitten capers, Felix closed his eyes, burrowed his nose into the crook of Jodie's arm, and went to sleep.

Jodie's mom paid Mrs. Dent, and Felix was put in the pet-carrying box they'd bought from the local pet shop on the way.

Jodie looked down at her sleeping kitten and smiled. "Look," she said. "He's so fluffy that you can hardly tell which is his head and which is his tail!"

"He does have a wonderful thick coat," Mrs. Dent agreed. "The thickest I've ever seen. You'll need a special comb for grooming him. And he'll need to be combed every day." She wrote down the details for Jodie.

Jodie thanked her and gave Felix a

gentle stroke before closing the carrying box.

Still sleeping, Felix purred. What a lovely life he was going to have with his new family. . . .

On the way home, Jodie and her mom popped into Pearce's Perfect Pets.

"Oh, you've brought your new kitten in to see me," said Mr. Pearce, the owner.

Felix allowed himself to be lifted out of his basket, put on the counter, and shown off to Mr. Pearce.

"Well!" said Mr. Pearce. "What a fine kitten—and such a wonderful coat."

Felix preened himself, purring loudly. He could get used to all this praise!

Jodie nodded, pleased. "He's adorable, isn't he?"

"You don't want to sell him, do you?" Mr. Pearce joked.

"No way!" Jodie said. "We've come in to buy a special comb for grooming long-haired cats." She gave Mr. Pearce

the piece of paper Mrs. Dent had given her, with the type of comb written on it.

"I don't think I've got one in stock," said Mr. Pearce. "But I'll order one for you. Jot down your phone number and I'll call you when it's in."

"I hope it won't take long," Jodie's mom said, writing down their number. "I want that gray fluff combed out before it gets shed all over the house!"

Mr. Pearce tickled Felix behind his ears. "With a thick coat like that, I bet you'll comb enough fur off him to knit yourself a wool sweater!" he joked.

Jodie laughed. "I just want to keep him looking good."

"I'll tell you what," Mr. Pearce said.

"He's such a handsome kitten that I'd like to take his photograph to put in my window. I'm sure it would attract a lot of attention. I'll give you the comb and a nice new collar in return. How's that?"

"Great!" said Jodie. "Can we, Mom?"

Mrs. Taylor nodded. "I don't see why not," she said.

Felix began to wash his face so that he'd look his best for the photo.

"Why don't you choose a collar while I go and get my camera?" said Mr. Pearce.

Jodie held a red and a green collar next to Felix, then chose the red one. She was carefully putting it on him when Mr. Pearce came back with his camera.

Felix just loved attention. Everyone in

the shop was watching him now. "How about this?" he purred, looking over his shoulder, his tail up straight. "Or this?" he meowed, rolling on his back and looking up at the camera, his blue eyes wide. "Have you ever seen anything so cute?"

"I think he knows what's going on," Mr. Pearce said, grinning. "He's posing like a model. He thinks he's one of those supermodels."

Supermodel? More like super*kitten*, Felix thought.

Chapter Three

"You'll have to try to keep Felix off this sofa, Jodie," Mrs. Taylor said a couple of days later.

Jodie had just come in from school and was watching TV with Felix on her lap.

Mrs. Taylor dabbed at the sofa with a damp cloth, then frowned at the gray fur she'd gathered up. "Dad sat down wearing his new suit and got it covered in gray hairs this morning," she went on.

"Sorry," Jodie said. "I'll try and brush some of the loose fluff out of Felix's coat later." She was going to make do with an old blue hairbrush until the special comb arrived at the pet shop.

Clicking her tongue a little under her breath, Mrs. Taylor went over to the vacuum cleaner in the corner. "And this old vacuum cleaner of ours is hopeless!" she added.

"Want me to try?" Jodie offered, feeling guilty at the extra work Felix's fur was making for her mom.

Mrs. Taylor shook her head. "It's much too heavy for you to lug around, honey. It's too heavy for me!" She plugged in the big old machine and switched it on.

Felix, who'd been snoozing, sat up suddenly. What was that horrible roaring noise? He jumped down and made a dash for the stairs. Pale gray fluff hung in the air as he ran. . . .

It was Saturday and Jodie was taking her time in the bathroom. She didn't have to rush to school this morning and could play with her new kitten all day.

Felix had decided to keep Jodie company while she showered, and was perched on the edge of the bathtub. He bobbed from side to side, dabbing his paw in the drops of water. "Why can't I catch these little round silvery things?" he meowed sharply. It was very annoying!

Jodie turned off the shower and put a dollop of soapy foam on the edge of the bath for Felix to play with.

Felix looked at the white froth. He reached out a paw—but the part he touched seemed to disappear. Very odd.

He leaned over to sniff the strange stuff—and jumped back in surprise, sneezing as tiny soapy bubbles flew up his nose. Felix lost his balance and slid into the bathtub, a wisp of foam still on his nose.

"Oh, Felix!" Jodie cried. "You silly thing!"

Jodie couldn't stop laughing as she lifted Felix out of the bath.

Then she noticed the hairs that had flown off Felix as he'd skidded into the bath. She grabbed a cloth and quickly wiped them up before her mom noticed. Jodie could hear the vacuum cleaner on again, downstairs.

Felix had been with the Taylors for just over a week now, and he had settled

in really well. But there was one big problem: his fur!

Felix's lovely thick coat shed oodles of fluffy hair wherever Felix went. And Mrs. Taylor was not pleased about it.

Jodie got dressed and took Felix into her bedroom. "Time to brush out some of that fluff," she said to him, setting him down on her bed.

She went to find the old blue hairbrush. But when she came back, Felix had vanished. Then she noticed a fluffy tail as fat as a squirrel's sticking out of the comforter. "I see you!" she called.

Jodie flung back the comforter to find Felix crouched down ready to pounce. He leaped into the air, scrabbled up

her back, and landed on her shoulder. "You're back! Let's play!" he meowed loudly.

As Jodie collapsed onto the bed, giggling, her mom appeared in the doorway.

"Just look at all that fluff on your bed, Jodie," Mrs. Taylor said frowning. "You'd better change the sheets. And don't you think it's about time you started grooming that kitten? If you combed out all that loose fur it wouldn't come out all over the house!"

"I'm going to, Mom—right now," Jodie said, and held up the brush to show her.

With a sigh, Mrs. Taylor went back to her cleaning. Pulling Felix onto her lap,

Jodie gently began to stroke the brush along his back.

But as far as Felix was concerned, the bristly blue creature was trying to attack him! He sprang round. "How dare you!" he hissed, ready to fight the brush.

Jodie sighed. "Come on, Felix, you have to let me groom you—otherwise we'll both be in trouble!"

Just then, the vacuum cleaner stopped again, and Mrs. Taylor called from the bathroom. "Jodie, leave that kitten alone for a moment and come in here, will you?"

Jodie put the brush down on the bed and went out to her mom. Felix pounced on the blue creature, biting and kicking it. "Caught you!" he growled happily.

"Have you had Felix in here with you?" Jodie's mom asked sternly when Jodie went into the bathroom.

Jodie nodded. "He likes to sit and watch me brush my teeth."

"I thought so," Mrs. Taylor said, "because there are hairs in the sink and on the towels." Mrs. Taylor shook her head. "Wherever I look there's a ball of gray fur!"

"But what can I do, Mom?" Jodie said. "Felix can't help shedding."

"I never seem to stop cleaning these days," Mrs. Taylor grumbled. "Not since Felix arrived." And then she stared at a toothbrush in horror. "That's it!" she cried. "There's cat hair on my tooth-brush!"

"Maybe the special comb we ordered from the pet shop will work," Jodie said.

Her mom nodded. "I hope so—I feel worn out with all the extra work."

Feeling guilty, Jodie escaped back to her bedroom and watched as Felix burrowed under her comforter again, leaving a cloud of gray fur behind him. She just hoped that Felix would allow her to use the new comb on him. If he didn't, she could see things getting very difficult. . . .

Chapter Four

A couple of days later, Jodie and her mom made their way to Pearce's Perfect Pets after school. Mr. Pearce had called to say the special comb was in.

As they approached the pet shop Jodie noticed that Felix's photograph was now in the window. "Oh, look, Mom!" she pointed. "There's Felix! Doesn't he look gorgeous?"

They both stopped and stared at the big photograph of Felix in the middle of the window display. He was wearing his new collar, with his head on one side, looking his cutest. A sign above the picture read:

Posh Pets Come to Pearce's

Mrs. Taylor nodded. "Yes, he looks lovely." Then she gave a little sigh. "But sometimes I can't help wishing that you'd chosen one of the short-haired kittens."

"Don't say that, Mom!" Jodie protested. "I love Felix. He's the most beautiful kitten in the world!"

"He's certainly the fluffiest!" said Mrs. Taylor. And then she smiled. "He is gorgeous, and I'm awfully fond of him. But he makes such a mess!"

As they went into the shop, Jodie looked once more at the beautiful photograph of Felix. Who would have thought that choosing the fluffiest kitten would cause so many problems?

*　　*　　*

"I wish you'd let me comb you, Felix!" Jodie said. "It might help with all the fluff, you know."

"Purreow!" Felix said. "I've decided I don't like those things called brushes and combs—they mess up my lovely fur."

Jodie had tried the special comb for long-haired cats for the first time yesterday. But it hadn't been a great success. Felix treated it just like the blue hairbrush.

As he rolled on the carpet, showing his soft fluffy tummy, Jodie put her hand out for the comb. Half-hiding it in her hand, she very gently combed down his tummy with it and collected some soft fur in its plastic teeth.

Felix sprang to life. That thing again! "Meow!" He jumped on it, caught it, and gave it a good bite.

"Oh, Felix!" Jodie cried, pulling the comb away from him. It already had tiny teeth marks in the handle, where Felix had attacked it yesterday. His kitten teeth were as sharp as needles.

"Oh, don't you want to play?" Felix meowed.

Jodie sighed as she heard the vacuum cleaner roaring away downstairs again. "Maybe you'll let me groom you when you get older," she said.

Felix stared up at her with his bright blue eyes. No, he didn't think so. . . .

Just then, the doorbell rang downstairs and the vacuum cleaner was hastily switched off. As Mrs. Taylor opened the door, Jodie could hear a very familiar voice. Then her mom called upstairs.

"Jodie! Mrs. Oberon's here. Come and say hello!"

Jodie gathered Felix up. "Mrs. Oberon

is organizing the school fair this year," she told him. "She's my teacher. She's a little strict—but really nice when you get to know her."

"Of course I'd be delighted to help at the school fair," Mrs. Taylor was saying as Jodie carried Felix into the living room. "Just let me know what you'd like me to do."

Mrs. Oberon was sitting on the sofa. "Oh, thank you!" she said. Then she smiled at Jodie. "Hello, Jodie—what a nice kitten!" she added, seeing Felix. "Maybe we should have a cat competition at the fair. He'd be a shoe-in!"

Felix purred with pleasure. He liked Mrs. Oberon.

Jodie and her mom showed Mrs. Oberon to the door, then waited until their guest had reached the front gate.

Suddenly, Mrs. Taylor gasped. "Oh no!"

"What?" Jodie asked, puzzled.

"Mrs. Oberon's skirt!" Mrs. Taylor whispered.

"What about it?" Jodie asked, even more puzzled. She hadn't noticed anything strange about it.

"Didn't you see?" said her mom, closing the door. "All down the back of it— gray fur!"

Jodie went into the living room to look at the sofa. There was fur all over the cushions again. She hurriedly tried to brush it off.

"I thought I told you not to let that kitten on the sofa!" Mrs. Taylor thundered.

Felix, who was still sitting on the sofa, took one look at Mrs. Taylor's angry face and disappeared underneath it.

"This is so embarrassing!" Jodie's mom went on. "What on earth will Mrs. Oberon think when she gets home and sees her skirt covered in fur?" Jodie didn't really think there was anything wrong with having cat fur on your skirt or on the carpet, the sofa, or in the bathtub. But her mom sighed heavily. "This is the last straw! I'm beginning to think that kitten of yours ought to live in the garage, you know."

"Mom!" Jodie protested. "We can't do that—he'd hate it!"

Felix, lying flat underneath the sofa, gave a frightened squeak. This was going too far! A kitten—a superkitten like him—couldn't possibly live in a garage.

"Well, I just can't think of another

solution," Mrs. Taylor said. "He refuses to be groomed, he won't stay off the furniture . . . and all I do is clean the place morning, noon, and night!"

"But, Mom—" Jodie was just about to start pleading with her mom when the phone rang.

"It's Bill Pearce," a voice said when Jodie answered it. "From Pearce's Perfect Pets. How's your fluffy kitten?"

"Er . . . he's okay," Jodie said, looking at her mom, who was still frowning and was about to start vacuuming again.

"And did the new comb do the trick?" Mr. Pearce asked.

"Not exactly," Jodie said uncomfortably.

"Well, it's about that—about the fur—

that I'm calling you," Mr. Pearce went on. "Can I have a word with your mom?"

Jodie handed the phone to Mrs. Taylor, who spoke to Mr. Pearce for a while.

Then she put the phone down, looking puzzled. "Mr. Pearce says that he has some people in the shop who want to meet Felix," she said.

Hearing his name, Felix gave a mew of alarm and crawled to the very back of the sofa. What was happening now?

"What's it about, Mom?" Jodie asked, surprised.

"He wouldn't say," Mrs. Taylor replied. "But they're coming over right away."

She switched on the vacuum cleaner. "It
all sounds very mysterious."

Chapter Five

"Hello," Jodie said shyly, as Mr. Pearce brought a small, smiling man and a tall woman with frizzy red hair into the house.

"This is Mr. Tompkins and his assistant, Ms. Spark," said Mr. Pearce.

"Pleased to meet you," said Jodie's mom, shaking hands with them. "Although I can't think why you wanted to meet Felix."

Felix was watching from underneath the sofa. What did these people want with him?

"If I may explain," Mr. Tomkins said, stepping forward. "My assistant, Ms. Spark here, visited Mr. Pearce's shop a few days ago and admired the photograph of Felix in the window. . . . "

With a soft meow, Felix came out from under the sofa. "Here I am!"

The two visitors gave an "Aaah!" of admiration.

"Oh, how sweet!" Ms. Spark cried. Her red curls bobbed round her pointy face. "Mr. Pearce told me that Felix was the fluffiest kitten he'd ever seen!" she said.

"And I'm pleased to see he's very fluffy indeed," Mr. Tomkins added.

Jodie picked up Felix and stroked him proudly. A small shower of gray fluff floated out from his coat. Everyone watched as it slowly sank to the floor. Jodie's heart sank too. Was her mom going to be angry?

"Ahem . . . " Ms. Spark cleared her throat. "Mr. Pearce also told me you were having some trouble with Felix's fur."

"Well, yes," said Mrs. Taylor. She glanced at Jodie. "It's true that all I seem to do these days is clean up after Felix. I've got a vacuum cleaner, but it's not really up to the job."

"And that is why we're here!" boomed Mr. Tomkins happily.

"Shall I go and get it, sir?" Ms. Spark asked, a hint of excitement in her voice.

Mr. Tomkins nodded. "If you don't mind, Ms. Spark."

Ms. Spark went to the white van parked outside. She came back in carrying a strange, shiny machine. Written on the side, in bright blue letters, was Wizard.

"It looks like a robot!" Jodie said, staring at the large silver box with arms attached.

Felix jumped down from Jodie's arms and approached the machine. What a strange-looking creature! He saw himself in the shiny surface. "Meeoww!" What a fine-looking kitten!

"This," said Mr. Tomkins proudly, "is my latest invention. It's not just a vacuum cleaner . . . "

Felix backed away from the silver creature. "Is that a vacuum cleaner?" he meowed.

"It's *the* vacuum cleaner!" Mr. Tomkins continued. "Better than any other!" He beamed at Jodie and her mom. "I've called it the Wizard because it can clean any house like magic!"

"Really?" Mrs. Taylor looked at it wistfully. "Well, it looks very good, but—"

Mr. Tomkins held up his hand. "Please allow us to demonstrate . . ." He turned to his assistant. "Ms. Spark, would you plug in the Wizard, please?"

"Certainly, Mr. Tomkins," his assistant replied. By now, Ms. Spark's red curls seemed to frizz with excitement.

Felix wondered if he should make a run for it. He'd heard the dreaded words "vacuum cleaner," and that usually meant trouble.

But while he was deciding, Ms. Spark switched the machine on. The silver creature began to hum.

Felix sat with his head on one side and stared, puzzled. Why wasn't it making a horrible loud roaring sound like Mrs. Taylor's vacuum cleaner?

Ms. Spark began to put the machine to work, moving one of its long rubbery arms over the sofa.

"Look at that!" Mrs. Taylor cried, delighted. The sofa cushions looked brand new!

Then Ms. Spark pushed the machine across the carpet. "With one gentle push, the Wizard slides easily along the floor, picking up every single hair as it passes," she said.

"It picks up fur you didn't know you had!" Mr. Tomkins joked.

Felix watched the humming silver creature gliding smoothly along the carpet. It didn't seem fierce, like the other vacuum cleaner. And he did like being able to see himself in the creature's shiny body. Maybe he should make friends with it.

Felix ran toward the machine, jumped on it, and pawed at his reflection.

"Felix looks as if he's driving it!" Jodie laughed.

Everyone smiled, watching Felix as he sat on the Wizard like a figurehead. His purring was almost as loud as the Wizard's hum.

As Ms. Spark steered the Wizard past Jodie, Felix looked up. "Hey, Jodie!" he meowed. "This is fun!"

Mrs. Taylor shook her head in awe,

looking at the spotless sofa and carpet. "I've never seen the place looking so clean," she said. "At least, not since Felix has been here."

Jodie had to agree.

"And finally," said Ms. Spark as she switched the vacuum cleaner off, "the Wizard also sucks fur and dust from the air—before it has a chance to settle."

"That's fantastic!" Jodie said.

As the machine stopped moving, Felix stepped off and sat next to his new friend, his head to one side.

Mr. Pearce began clapping. "It looks as though Felix thinks he's done the cleaning himself," he said.

"He's an absolute darling!" Ms. Spark cried.

Felix was really enjoying himself. Everyone seemed to think he was great! And now that his silver friend had cleaned up all his fur, perhaps Mrs. Taylor would forget about banishing him to the garage.

But Jodie's mom was looking worried again. "It's a marvelous machine," she said. "I'd love one—but I'm afraid we simply can't afford a new vacuum cleaner. Especially such an expensive-looking one. . . . "

"Oh, I don't want you to buy one!" Mr. Tomkins said.

Chapter Six

"What?" Mrs. Taylor said in surprise.

"Let me explain," said Mr. Tomkins. "We want Felix to star in our advertisements," he said.

Jodie gasped.

"He's a natural," Mr. Tomkins went on. "With Felix showing off the Wizard, we'll sell thousands!"

"Oh, wow!" Jodie cried. She picked

up Felix and hugged him. "You're going to be famous!" she whispered.

Felix rubbed his head against Jodie's neck. "Great!" he purred. "I've always wanted to be a superkitten."

"I can see the posters now," Mr. Tomkins said, rubbing his hands together happily. "They'll say: buy a Wizard—the ultimate furbuster!"

"Or how about: so quiet it won't even frighten a kitten!" Ms. Spark added.

"Very good, Ms. Spark!" Mr. Tomkins boomed.

"And: so light even a kitten can push it!" Mr. Pearce offered. "If you don't mind me joining in," he added, going a bit red.

"Thank you, Mr. Pearce! Another

excellent suggestion!" cried Mr. Tomkins. Then he turned to Jodie's mom. "We'll pay a fee, of course. And the 'Wizard Kitten' must have a Wizard for his own home. We'll leave this one for you."

Jodie and her mom stood there, too astounded to speak. Felix gave a short meow. "Say yes!" He wanted to be a superkitten. He wanted to be famous— and he wanted it now!

One evening, a few weeks later, Jodie and her parents were all sitting in front of the television. Felix was sitting on Jodie's lap. He was quite a bit bigger, but still very fluffy.

"Mr. Tomkins said it would be on at

five-thirty," Jodie said. She looked at her watch. "It's almost time."

"My watch says twenty-five past," Mr. Taylor said.

Felix looked up at Jodie, his bright blue eyes puzzled. Why was everyone so excited? Even Jodie's dad had

come home from work early.

"Is the VCR set?" Mrs. Taylor asked.

Just then there was a noise outside in the hall and a cheerful woman poked her head around the door. It was Mrs. Bell.

Felix turned around and meowed. Ever since Mr. Tomkins had paid a lot of money for Felix's kitten modeling, Mrs. Bell had been coming here to do all the cleaning.

"I've finished cleaning upstairs," Mrs. Bell said. "Do you want me to do in here now?"

"Oh, Mrs. Bell," said Jodie's mom, smiling. "Come and watch the commercial first! It should be on any min—"

She was interrupted by a scream from Jodie. "Here he is! Oh, look, Felix, there you are!"

Jodie held Felix up in front of the television and he saw himself sitting proudly on a Wizard.

"Solve even the fluffiest problem with the air of your Wizard!" said a voice on the TV. "Cleans your home like magic!"

"Don't you look gorgeous!" Jodie cried.

"Purreow!" said Felix. He jumped down and sat as close to the TV as he could, staring up at himself. "Yes, I do look pretty good . . . "

As the commercial ended, everyone sighed with pride. Then Felix gave a tiny sneeze and shook himself, sending a shower of fluffy gray fur into the air.

Jodie laughed. "You can do that as much as you like, Felix!" she said. "Because now you're getting paid for it!"

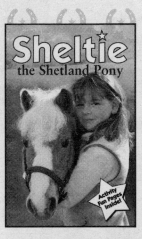